Eighteen

Sandy Steinman

BLUE LIGHT PRESS
1st WORLD
PUBLISHING

San Francisco | Fairfield | Delhi

Eighteen

Sandy Steinman

Copyright ©2023 by Sandy Steinman

First Edition.

ISBN: 978-1-4218-3537-2

Library of Congress Cataloging-in-Publication Data

1ST WORLD LIBRARY
PO Box 2211
Fairfield, Iowa 52556
www.1stworldpublishing.com

BLUE LIGHT PRESS
www.bluelightpress.com
Email: bluelightpress@aol.com

TABLE OF CONTENTS

Eighteen

EIGHTEEN

It wasn't only my father. It was my mother, my grandmother, all my aunts, my piano teacher, Mrs. Kramer, Rabbi Benjamin and even the kosher butcher. Everyone told me I had to marry by eighteen.

"That's the cutoff," said Grandma.

"Marry rich," instructed my father, "and fast," fearing I'd fade after eighteen. Mother had married at eighteen as had his mother. If I waited, I wouldn't be a good catch. All the prized beauties were snapped up early.

"Maybe, God forbid, deflowered," worried my father, marked down in value, like the end-of-season coats in his ladies-wear store: 20% to 50% off. Instead of catching a doctor, I'd have to settle for a salesman, like him, or even a bouncer.

"Marry tall," advised Mother, professing short men had low self esteem and they bragged, interrupted, and bought big flashy cars in vulgar colors. Daddy was tall. My brothers were tall.

"Tall and handsome," was Mother's prerequisite.

All my aunts married tall, even Aunt Marge, who was shy and gargled when she laughed. She was twenty and reluctant when pushed into marriage, with equally unwilling Uncle George, who was tall, had a voice like a buzz saw, and sold shoes at Macy's.

Aunt Shirley was barely eighteen when she married tall Uncle Arthur to keep him safe at home during World War II, but he got sent off to France anyway and stayed five years.

1

One night, while he was gone, Aunt Shirley slept over. Alone in the kitchen, as we ate bowls of rice pudding, Aunt Shirley whispered that the sex part wasn't so hot. "What's all the fuss about?" she wailed. "I don't get it."

I was eight years old at the time and an attentive listener. I shrugged my shoulders. I didn't get it either.

When I was seventeen, I asked Mother, "Don't I have any say?"

"No," she told me, "Old maid status is automatically awarded at twenty-one, a shameful taboo."

As I approached eighteen, I stood in the bathroom fretting into the mirror, inspecting myself for telltale signs.

It was true. I'd lost my bloom! I knew my father saw it, and that he shivered at the prospect of being stuck with me for life. One afternoon, he brought home Harvey Shapiro, a short tailor with blackheads in his ears.

That spurred me to quickly look around and find someone myself, but I simply couldn't decide. I wandered from one to another unpromising prospect like a blindfolded guest at a children's party, unable to resolve where to pin the tail on the donkey.

Sheldon was short. Robert had a dead tooth in the front. Morris was a Mama's boy, and James snorted when he laughed.

Suave Alfred didn't go for me, but Paul from Pittsburgh did. He dazzled me singing in perfect pitch, and he had a hamster named Twitchy. Seven months later, at the altar we pledged, "we do."

Sixty-eight years are gone now, and we still "do."

VANITY

My mother was beautiful and vain. She took hours to dress for a party. Her attractiveness was her trademark. I didn't see it. I wouldn't have known she was beautiful if it wasn't for the parade of well-wishers at a social event, perhaps a wedding, or a Bar Mitzvah, that would greet me crooning, "You must be so proud to have such a beautiful mother."

I didn't see it. What I did see was Mother beautifying herself, the hours she spent primping in front of her dressing room's full-length mirror. Mother would stick her tongue out a little and strike poses, as if trying to seduce herself.

Mother's grooming was impeccable. She had elegant jars of smelly potions and lotions she swore by. Her perfumes had dramatic names: Joy, Jealousy, Euphoria.

Mother had two aversions – body hair and arithmetic. Body hair wasn't dainty. She shaved her legs and her underarms daily, and every week used a hot wax depilatory to remove her moustache. As for arithmetic, she believed it wasn't feminine to add and subtract and refused to balance her checkbook, claiming my father enjoyed doing it.

One day, Mother decided to experiment with the hot wax on her underarm hair. Her routine was to heat the wax until it melted and use a tongue depressor to coat her upper lip. When the wax hardened and cooled, with one yank, she pulled it off.

On the day she planned to wax her underarms, she padded into the bathroom with the pan of hot wax and locked the door. She dabbed the hot wax on her underarms with the tongue depressor. When the wax hardened it began to pull. Soon it became terribly painful. She had to hold her arms in the air.

She screamed, "Help!" My father heard her screaming and called the fire department. Three burly men arrived in a flash with hatchets and hammers and broke down the bathroom door. There stood Mother with no clothes on and her arms high in the air.

I've always wondered how she got the wax off.

PERFORMANCE

"You look beautiful, dear."

Miranda stood at the mirror trembling in her lemon velvet gown, Mother's favorite. She was tense: primed to perform at the signal.

"Deep breaths, dear, head erect."

Spotlight blinded and weary from endless rehearsals, Miranda scanned the audience clutching her elbow-length gloves.

"Calm yourself, Miranda. Remember to smile

Mother sat at her usual perch, first row center, alone and silent amidst the audience babble. Her heavy jade earrings shuddered above her shoulders. She seemed poised as when she was alive, easy to spot with her perennially petulant stare.

"It's my trademark," she'd boasted.

Tonight, Mother's sunken cheeks were tinted a pastel mosaic of tiny hearts and her nostrils emitted pale purple steam. No one appeared to notice. A silver glow haloed her red velvet cloche.

"No need to be frightened, dear."

Pretending Mother had winked at her, Miranda flung a kiss and a wave at the audience as Mother impatiently flipped the program's pages.

At last, the signal – the conductor gave a short tap with his baton. The audience hushed as Miranda twirled across the stage and flawlessly belted out several romantic show tunes — hers and Mother's favorites, "Some Enchanted Evening." After that, "Bewitched."

Minutes later, with a deep curtsy to the audience, Miranda beamed the blazing professional smile Mother had long ago taught her.

Thunderous applause.

COLOR IN THE GARDEN

"When change occurs, a window opens to growth." I nodded in agreement, though I wasn't quite sure what the woman meant. "And growth is always welcome, isn't it?"

"Of course," I replied, and hired the prospective new gardener, though I was still unsure what she meant by change and growth.

It wasn't until months later that I discovered exactly what she had in mind by what she set into the ground in the streaming sun of my kitchen garden.

"What I want is vibrant color," I explained during the interview. She nodded, sitting tall and straight at my kitchen table as if rooted into the oak chair. She sipped geranium tea while tapping a shiny spade on her knee.

"I like the vibrant primary hues to excite my eyes," I told her, "heady perfume to stimulate my senses as I gaze out into the garden through my open window, drying dishes or preparing a summer's ratatouille." I pointed sadly at the bland callas, boring white impatiens, white hydrangeas, tree roses.

It's not that I have an aversion to white. I prefer white sheets on our feather bed, white towels, white underwear. Jasmine rice, filet of sole, and vanilla ices are favored dinner fare. I attend with joy the chaste weddings of a first marriage and celebrate the Chinese New Year. Yet, white in the garden depresses me.

"I have the perfect solution," she announced, and on her next scheduled workday, she arrived with twenty skinny pale green stalks. "Spanish Manandola Lilies," she announced, "from my stepmother's garden. Ten are vivid red, ten, sunny yellow." She had an odd expression on her face, a smirk, perhaps a near-wicked smile, as though she held an amusing, dark secret.

At the front of the embankment where the slope is shallow, she dug deep and planted ten slim stalks announcing they would be red blooms. Down below the knotted pine steps, she planted the yellows.

I was intrigued. "How tall will they grow?"

Shrugging her wide shoulders and flashing that odd smile, she replied in a whisper, "Very, very tall."

Several weeks later, after removing the remaining white periwinkle, she announced that she had made some significant life changes. Uprooting her present husband, she'd plucked a new boyfriend who was flying with her to Paris.

"Besides, my work here is done." she said with her strange smile.

Today at the kitchen sink, as warm water foams the detergent, I see thick pale green stalks out the window, thick as young elm trunks. Squinting, I gaze up at the Manandola Lilies, now 70 feet tall. They are still growing. Buds have not yet appeared. I will need strong binoculars to see the bright yellow and red blossoms, if they ever bloom.

GEORGE THE TURTLE

I lied when I promised Grandma I wouldn't dig up George again. Yet last night, same as the night before, I tiptoed downstairs while she slept and dug him out of his tiny grave under the forsythia near the swings. Last month, little Timmy had bathed George in a sink of scalding water. He didn't mean to hurt him.

When Grandma heard I'd done it again, she sent me to my room. "God is angry."

"I wanted a last peek, Grandma."

"God commands we must not desecrate graves."

Annoyed, I punched my pillow and decided to kill Stanley Popkin, formerly my friend. I trusted Stanley, told him not to tell Grandma, but he did.

He marched up the porch steps where Grandma sat folding clothes.

"Susan's Grandma," he screamed. "She dug George up again."

I'll kill Stanley, give him ant poison. He'll die. Wait! I'll have no one to play with. Me and Stanley play kick the can after naptime.

Maybe I'll hit him with a brick. Not a hard brick. Maybe punch him in the arm. Gently. Or I won't share my snack. Or tell him stuff. That's it. I won't tell him stuff.

The scabs on my knees itch tonight, resting on the cool ground as I uncover George once more, remove him from his tiny grave.

His shell is soft. His head rests on my thumb with its torn nail. I stroke him, same as when I placed him in that soil, wondering when God will take him or change him into somebody else.

THE PRIZE WINNER

Sheila Jones gleefully waves the fifth grade spelling bee prize. Snorting, her angry teacher, Mrs. Shreiber, tightly squeezes the prize winner's skinny shoulder with her fat manicured hand. She forces a smile for the camera. The two have despised each other since fourth grade when Mrs. Shreiber called Sheila liar and a cheat in front of the class, claiming Sheila didn't dot an "i" on the spelling test.

"But, Mrs. Shreiber, I did dot that "i."

"Don't give me those innocent eyes, Sheila." Mrs. Shreiber points to Sheila's spelling paper. "You dotted the "i" after Sydelle took off credit and gave your paper back."

Sheila feels ashamed even though she didn't do anything wrong. She is sure that she dotted all the "i"s. If her perfect spelling record is broken, she won't win the fifth grade weekly spelling bee prize.

Sydelle must be jealous. She never wins anything. That's probably why she took the point off. "Look Sydelle, there's the dot. See it?"

"You sneaked it in when you got your paper back." Sydelle whirls around so fast, her fat braid smacks Sheila in the face.

Sheila is nervous going up to Mrs. Shreiber's desk to tell her that Sydelle was mistaken. Old fat face with her stupid Shirley Temple ringlets probably won't believe her.

"A liar and a cheat!" the teacher yells, right in front of the whole class.

Holding in tears, Sheila runs to the coat closet and grabs her coat. She dashes out of the classroom, out the heavy school door, runs down Bedford Avenue clutching her spelling paper, fleeing home to tell her mother. "Miss Shreiber called me a liar," she sobs.

Mother shoots her surprise face at Sheila. "So you left school? You just walked out?"

The telephone rings. It's Mr. Beisham, the principal. Mother talks a minute, then she grabs her coat and Sheila's hand. "Come, Sheila."

Ten minutes later they are in the principal's office with Mrs. Shreiber.

"I never called her that," says Mrs. Shreiber.

"Boy," Sheila tells Mr. Beisham, "What a liar!" Mr. Beisham scolds the embarrassed and contrite Mrs. Shreiber.

Today, Sheila's blouse blazes with four bird pins commemorating four previous wins: a robin, a bluejay, an eagle and a parrot. Mrs. Shreiber, reluctant, yet resolved, pins a New Guinea Babbler on Sheila, who flashes a toothy grin.

MR. RIGHT

It's 6 A.M. and already sweltering. When the alarm rings, Julia quickly silences it. She feeds the mewing cats, whisking them outside while carting in her suitcase, hidden under the porch.

Elias, Julia's fifth husband, sleeps on. Arms flung out, huge belly high in the air, he hoards the bed. His frizzy red hair is mussed. Julia resists combing through it. In his white silk pajamas, he looks innocent as an altar boy. Julia loves his hair, loves him when asleep, as she did the others, even ferret-faced Vernon, with his alligator temperament.

Silently, she pads into the kitchen, whispers into the phone, "Ready in minutes, Christopher."

"It's a pattern," Dr. Hongo had suggested. "I am keenly aware that your nuptial interest fades a few months into marriage."

Julia was doubtful. "Elias bores me."

"I've heard your complaints before, Julia," Dr. Hongo looked at his notes. "Doubtless, you are afflicted with a compulsion. Always leave at daybreak while they sleep"

"Compulsion? Nonsense. I simply haven't found Mr. Right."

Now combed and dressed, Julia lifts garden shears from the drawer, adds a drop of oil, wipes the blades thoroughly. Tiptoeing to the head of the bed, she reaches down, carefully clips a thick lock of Elias's hair, placing it in a zip-lock baggy. Elias wrinkles his nose

13

and turns over. She opens her suitcase, adds the baggy to four others. Closing it, blowing silent kisses to Elias, she carries the bag to the porch.

NOT GUILTY

When Anna Cohen visited her dentist, long overdue, he somberly announced that because of her negligence and the resulting grievous deterioration, he had to extract all her teeth and remove her gums and chin. But, if we act quickly," he assured her, "with luck, patience and my uncommon skill, I'll save your neck."

Dr. Familant believed he could reconstruct Anna's face with nylon chicken wire. "And you can wear tooth falsies," he claimed, "tiny, straight, and pearly-white."

Anna was dubious.

"They'll look terrific," he insisted. "A marked improvement over your common-variety teeth, which are crooked, crammed, and of a mahogany hue."

In the middle of the blockbuster extraction, Anna was overcome by the nitrous oxide. Her brain shut down for a quarter hour. When she recovered her senses, she was afflicted with aphasia, save calling out random adjectives.

"Fluorescent." "Hapless." "Strapless."

Sadly, Dr. Familant was unable to wire poor Anna back to normalcy. She remained toothless, gumless and chinless. The next week her cheeks caved in. Anna, who had always been remarkably re-sourceful, concealed her disability, wearing a large red kerchief under her nose. She tied it behind her head like a cowboy bandit.

"Extreme." "Fluffy." "Penitent."

She soon became a popular guest on TV talk shows, due to her curious appearance and unique responses to the host's questions.

"Felicitous." "Glib." "Kinky."

After a few months, Anna chose a new and more lucrative vocation. She was hired as the sole fore-person for the endless barrage of court TV trials, mistrials, and retrials that had become a permanent feature of western culture. Thus, she spent the rest of her days popping up periodically when the judge called, "Madame fore-person, what say you?"

"Gritty," Anna would call out. "Silty," "Not Glittery."

DINNER PARTIES

Arrange a dinner party? The thought throws me into a panic. As if it's a catastrophe if the sterling silver sugar scuttle was displayed unpolished, and the police would haul me off, charge me with "tarnish," and toss me into the slammer.

Dinner parties? Days of preparation, polishing silver, scrubbing the bathroom, washing windows, displaying new guest towels, shopping for exotic ingredients to prepare fancy recipes from gourmet magazines for fussy friends.

A dinner party is like opening night of a Broadway show. The hostess is leading lady, stage manager, playwright, director, and producer. Doubtless, she'll suffer opening night jitters. Perhaps she will forget her lines or misplace the props. Perhaps the guests will arrive cranky or allergic, or God forbid, vegan!

I've inherited "Dinner Party Anxiety" from Mother, who awarded me her artistic temperament with high standards for performance, but she had no taste for light comedy. Her parties were tragedy: *Othello, Macbeth, Death of a Salesman.* She directed with wringing hands.

As a child, my role was lowly stagehand. "Not the ceramic goblets, Sondra. The crystal goblets." I'd set and reset the table while she fretted in her ritual quest for perfection. At dress rehearsal, we'd both be in a frenzy, which for some reason, quieted her. "Being nervous before a performance is good," she'd console me, her eyes twitching.

Mother was a gold star cook. Her roast chicken always got rave reviews. "Better than Aunt Dora's!" my uncles bellowed.

Today, my roast chicken matches hers. Along with panic, I've inherited Mother's talent for cooking. But please, in my house, let's forget formality. No silver, crystal, lace or china. Let's potluck, come as you are and relax. Let's eat in the kitchen.

THE COIF-OFF

At Rumplemeyers, purchasing caramels for Cousin Judith's graduation, a tiny man, no taller than Pamela, my nine year old, tapped my shoulder.

"Ahem, Madame. I am Mario LaRusso." His heavily accented voice was melodic. "Your coiffure is intriguing." He whipped out a card. "I am a hairdresser."

After small bits of chaff, he suggested we stop for tea. We sat at a Schrafft's booth. He leaned across, playfully tousling my hair, and whispered, "Shall we have an affair?

His shiny leather boots had three-inch heels. "You might pick on someone your own size." I sniffed.

He glared. "I'm almost five feet."

"A pee wee."

"Fortunately, we're the same size seated." Winking, he said something in Italian. I laughed, pretending to understand.

"A pot of Earl Grey, please," I told the waiter.

"In the old country, short men are sought after," he said. "Their virility is legendary. Practically all the sensuous women try to seduce them. Most of the men are arrogant and fussy. They only choose the youngest and prettiest. The women know they must be careful and protect themselves. They choose only the most trustworthy lovers, who will hide them and can keep secrets. This is crucial because if the women are caught, the villagers stone them."

"Tomorrow I sail for Paris. Why not come along? I will introduce you as Miss Tress."

I was intrigued. Could I miss sewing circle? Find a nursemaid for Pamela? Would Nigel swallow my yarn that Cousin Jan invited me to her spa?

"I'll see."

"Meet me here tomorrow at six." He caressed my hair.

I arrived exhilarated, having hired a nursemaid and duped Nigel. I sat alone until closing. No sign of Mario. At home I found a note under the door.

"From Mario," it read. The rest was in Italian. I don't understand Italian, so I tore it up.

WORLD TRAVELER

Helen left her chocolate cherries in my car. She's back from a Tonga Earth Watch project; the Giant Clams had stopped reproducing. Yesterday, I treated her to lunch, a post celebration of her eighty-fifth birthday.

"What did you do in Tonga?"

"We beat drums, but what helped most was planting the clams in circles so they could stimulate one another. They're bisexual, you know." She giggles.

"Keep the candy," she tells me on the phone.

"S'good."

"I'll bring another box if you invite me to dinner next week before I fly to Alaska."

"Alaska?"

I'd be more astonished if it weren't Helen. Nothing stops Helen. Yesterday, over the Marvin Garden's birthday lunch, pasta bouncing from her fork, she reported that her Parkinson's has improved with the new medication.

"But it makes me wheeze. I'm dizzy as a butterfly and weak. Not a perfect solution, but the tremors are better. Hooray!"

Spaghetti flying.

We hold hands walking at the Farmers Market and buy bok choy, blueberries and lemon curd.

"Dip strawberries." She adjusts her flowered sunbonnet. "Bananas."

In her Civic Center Social Worker days, she headed the Home-makers Division. Perhaps that's where her inventive food suggestions come from. Or was it from her Kansas farm girlhood?

Never married. "Everyone teased my father." she told me one August night many years ago. "They said he planted his face on me at birth." We were in a Maine University dormitory at Presque Isle. Helen introduced me to Elderhostel the summer I turned forty.

"He was not pretty." She whirls and strikes a pose. "But don't I have a beautiful figure?"

Until the Parkinson's she prided herself in her agility and performed gymnastic stunts for the 32 Japanese students we co-hosted some twenty years ago.

At restaurants, she pockets used tea bags, butter pats and packets of Equal, yet manages thousand dollar contributions to Friends of the Earth.

"You're walking better now," I assure her. Her dry hand squeezes mine.

"Holding warm hands helps more than my cold cane."

So she's leaving for Alaska – Earth Watch again. This time it's the Caribou and Musk Oxen that need rescuing.

Why won't Helen rest on her sunny deck among the reeds of the Santa Venetia Canal? Study the herons and egrets we photographed many years ago?

"Death will have to hunt me down." she chuckles. "Where will he find me? She reaches over to open her top kitchen drawer, pulls out her map of the world and unfolds it. After a few minutes of serious study, she announces, grinning, "perhaps in the Himalayas. Maybe I'll fall from a yak."

At dinner over a dessert of chocolate cherries, I listen patiently to her endless slogans and reams of memorized poems.

"I'm intolerant of intolerance. Prejudiced against prejudice."

"It's never too late to have a happy childhood." A giggle.

Tumors. Tremors. Trouble walking. I remember when her retina detached in the steamy Amazon jungle five years ago, while at a construction project for an infant monkey orphanage.

A calamity? Not to Helen. An inconvenience.

YOU CAN'T TAKE IT WITH YOU

When my lonely, still lovely, actress, artist, mother, widowed twenty-five years, reached seventy-seven, she lived alone in a Manhattan studio, six floors up.

She claimed she loved the excitement of the city, the museums, theatres, restaurants and would never leave. Yet, she rarely ventured out, except mornings to the bank and occasional afternoons to Bernard Bolle's Beauty Salon. There, the faithful Bernard tinted her hair a honey shade, while his wife, Magdalena, matched it with polish, manicuring her nails.

My plane landed late, and Mother wasn't there to meet me. I waited two hours in the luggage room, then worried and anxious, phoned her apartment. She picked up with a cheerful hello.

Relieved, I scolded, "Why didn't you meet me at the airport as you always do?"

"I forgot and took a nap."

"I called you yesterday to verify my arrival time. Don't you remember?"

"Did you?"

Irritated, struggling with heavy luggage and birthday presents I'd hoped she'd help carry, I took the shuttle at the airport and walked from Grand Central the two long blocks to her tiny apartment. After

I rang for several minutes, she met me at the door. She stood there shivering, wrapped in a thin faded green and white striped towel, her thin wet hair clinging to her small head.

"I was in the bath."

Unpacked, baffled, I distracted myself at the window, listening to the city's moan curiously blending with the comedy show blaring on her TV. Below the sooty window were the street's endless honking trucks. A creeping yellow cab stopped in front of the apartment lobby, delivering the same skinny Chassid as last year, to the aging whore in apartment 4B.

After I followed Mother into her small shabby apartment, she dried her hair and dressed. Meanwhile, I poked around her tiny kitchen to find something for our lunch. I discovered bare cupboards except for one can of Campbell's tomato soup. The refrigerator was empty except for a can of Coca-Cola.

"Shall we go out for lunch?" I called into the closed bathroom door.

Immediately, the door flew open. With a whoop and a grin, Mother and asked, "Can we go to PJ's? It's right across the street, a busy cafeteria, always crowded. It was your uncle Dave's favorite. Movie stars eat there."

Her joy about going out for lunch delighted me. She was animated and smiling, a huge contrast to her former depressed demeanor.

In just a few minutes, she grabbed her rumpled and stained old coat and called out, "Let's go!"

An hour later, weary after our lunch at P.J. Clarke's, Mother lay reading on her frayed, cream chaise lounge in a lacy pink peignoir, hair tinted Autumn Peach with ever matching newly polished nails. She read and reread playbills, hundreds, saved over sixty years: George S. Kaufman, Edna Ferber, Moss Hart, her favorite, a former sweetheart and admirer.

Did she notice that the thin apple green wall-to-wall carpet was filthy and torn, that the formerly graceful ivory armoire, gilded in gold, tilted dangerously on wobbly curved legs?

"I got it at cost from Max M." she claimed proudly. Max, once her decorator, was now a dutiful friend, but like the other friends of years past, he'd recently moved from his Manhattan apartment to his daughter's Connecticut home and rarely called. Many of Mother's friends had moved, some to warmer climes: Florida. California. Others now lived in distant suburban retirement communities. Some had died.

She didn't seem to notice that black mascara ringed her frightened eyes, that her formerly perfectly applied pancake makeup, Max Factor, Natural Number Two, streaked her cheeks, that the bright orange Estee Lauder lipstick spidered down her chin.

She didn't know that ten years later, she'd no longer live in a Manhattan studio, but would reside 3000 miles west of P.J. Clarke's, housed with ten others, all missing memories, in a bedroom for three at a Care Center. Her hair, now foamy white, would be washed and set, nails still peach polished at Fanny's Beauty Shop.

"Who are you?" she asks the beauty parlor owner, Fanny, but doesn't seem to listen to the answer. The gentle Fanny shrugs, strokes Mother's tissue-thin cheek. Now toothless, Mother smiles.

"Mom, Moss Hart sent this to you," teases my brother, offering a box of caramel candies to my frail mother, who had refused lasagna at dinner.

"Moss Hart?" Mother snatches the box. "I better eat these now. Did you know?" she grins, "Moss Hart wrote a play that he called, "You Can't Take It with You?"

THE STAR OF APPLEGATE

In the game room she pets the dog, slurs toothless coos to cats, waltzes and twirls to tunes on TV, curtsies to applause and stares.

She squeezes close to her daughter, clutches a cashmere sleeve with trembling hand. "For the life of me, I know you, don't I? What's your name again?"

A lifelong yearning to be an actress: Auditions. Rehearsals. Costumes. Ovations.

Oohs at famous names.

At the fashion mall, posing, she points to mannequins echoing words from long gone days when girdled and coiffed, she shopped Henri Bendel. "I like that line. Those narrow pleats. That jacket length. That shade of green. Divine!"

Now swaddled in Depends, shocking pink jump suit, bold red coat, orange hair, she teeters in Reeboks, royal blue.

Clerk at an ice cream stand: "What'cha like today, lady?"

"Ethel Barrymore," she replies, "unless you have Tennessee Williams in a sugar cone?"

AS HE WAS

Thursday, at midnight, I'm jolted awake by my father's ghost. "Go to the darkroom," he whispers. "Duplicate me ten times."

I leave my bed, creep barefoot to the enlarger. "These prints must be incontrovertibly identical." He wags a skeletal finger. "One each for your mother, you children, your children, my sisters. Use black and white fiber-based paper, please: double-weight, eight by ten."

He smiles, vanishes.

The prints don't look like him. Wavy red hair, green eyes, tiny brown freckles translate poorly in zones of gray. Yet, his teaser's smile, tilted stance, head held too far forward – amazingly the same.

Trancelike in the darkroom, I swiftly lift slippery prints in porcelain trays with delicate tongs to the rhythm of the time-o-lite. It's like a ritual communion, a form of prayer. I stand attentive, shivering in the damp sour room, bathed under golden safelight, as I expose him. I wonder if he misses the Saratoga Springs trotters where my Brownie shot the photo.

"If only you could have borne the small losses, Dad. Cut back from two packs of Camels, your half pint of Jack Daniel's, two sets of singles." The doctor had ordered bed rest to repair his damaged heart. "I wanted to know you longer."

Raging, I reduce his proud six feet to ten inches, creating a false image: colorless, two dimensional. Then his smile appears in the tray. First faint highlights, then shadows deepen.

A FOR ARMAND

I can't wait for breakfast to be over. After I finish my cornflakes and orange juice and get combed and scrubbed, Mommy crosses me at Bedford Avenue and I go to kindergarten. I'll color with crayolas, finger paint, march around the room, and swing outside on the swings.

I have a boyfriend, Armand Lopez. He's got thick black lashes, and he's an artist. When he colors pictures in a coloring book, he stays inside the lines, and when he paints a yellow rose, it looks like a yellow rose. I like to watch him make a cursive capital "A." A for Armand.

I can't wait for kindergarten to be over today because Armand Lopez is swinging on the jungle gym with Roberta Rappaport and not me. Mrs. Kramer yelled at me for pushing Roberta and told me to stop singing "The Farmer in the Dell." What's wrong with singing "The Farmer in the Dell?" I like to sing.

"The Farmer in the Dell, The Farmer in the...." I only got two graham crackers at snack time, and Armand Lopez gave his to Roberta Rappaport, so she got four, and they won't let me in their club. I can't wait to go home so I can sing "The Farmer in the Dell."

I can't wait for supper. I'm sooo hungry. I only got two graham crackers snack time.

I can't wait for supper to be over. Salmon croquettes? Noodle kugel? Orange Jell-O for dessert? Blah!

Then I get to play "Fish" with Daddy.

It's bedtime? Already?

I can't wait for morning to peek into my Venetian blinds, the sun making stripes on my arm, and the birds singing outside. I'm going to wear my blue velvet skirt I got for Grandma's birthday party. Armand Lopez says blue is his favorite color.

I can't wait for breakfast to be over, because when I finish, I get to go see Armand Lopez.

I can't wait. I can't.

I can't.

SEYMOUR AND SANTA

I keep trying to make my friend Colleen understand that Jewish families don't celebrate Christmas. Even hearing talk about mangers or crèches makes my mother twitch and change the subject.

I plead with my father, "Can't we have a tree, Daddy? We could hang paper dreidels on the branches for decoration and put a Jewish star on top."

"Twelve years old and you're still asking for trees?" My father sighs. "How many times do I have to tell you that we Jews do not drag home trees and we don't worship false Messiahs."

"But Jesus was Jewish, Daddy."

My father snorts. He rolls his eyes and shrugs his shoulders. The subject is closed.

I just don't get it about Christmas. Who wouldn't want to be like everyone else in the world and have a twinkling tree with branches hanging over big fat presents, like bicycles and skateboards?

I like to sing Christmas carols, and I want to fit in. Hanukkah isn't as much fun. I never can remember what we are celebrating. Every year I look it up again in the Book of Knowledge.

A few days before Christmas last year, on a freezing Friday after-noon, Mother took my little brother Seymour and me to the toy section of Goldman's Department Store on Nostrand Avenue in Brooklyn. Seymour had sniffles and was cranky. Mother asked me to stay with him and let him play with the toys while she went to Ebinger's Bakery for challah and rugalach.

Seymour was climbing in and out of a shiny red wagon when a man dressed in a Santa Claus costume appeared out of nowhere down the tricycle aisle. He strolled over to Seymour, jingling bells, knelt down on one knee grinning, and handed him a candy cane.

"And what would you like Santa to bring you, my little man?"

Seymour began to scream. "No. No. You mustn't talk to me. You mustn't give me something." His little chin trembled as he pushed the candy cane back into the Santa's white-gloved hand. "I'm not allowed."

I saw the familiar dark stain traveling down his leggings. "I'm Jewish.

A few minutes later Mother returned. Seymour was still wailing, snot and drool dripping from his chin as I struggled to wipe his face with a soggy Kleenex.

Mother raised a fist and yelled across the store to Mr. Goldman. "Giving in to the Goyim, Goldman? Employing a Santa Claus? What kind of a Jew are you?"

Everyone in the store stared at her as she bellowed, "You're a traitor to your people."

A few days later, Seymour and I are invited to dinner at Colleen's house. Her father folds his hands, closes his eyes and we all bow our heads in prayer. He says a blessing to "Jesus Christ, Our Lord," and we all say "Amen," even Seymour, who doesn't seem to mind Jesus as much as Santa Claus.

TACTICS

I am frugal, the child of shameless spendthrifts. I was barely out of diapers when Mom and Dad taught me alibis for the department stores: Lord and Taylor, Saks Fifth Avenue, Bloomies. They'd put me on the phone with some cockamamie explanation for Mom's astronomical balance. I would be coached to sob, "Daddy's broken his hand," or "Mother can't leave Grandma's hospital bed."

Needless to say, the new full-length ranch mink, the Henredon dining room set, and the Cartier diamond earrings were reclaimed by the stores and carted away. I was left understandably insecure. To this day I always have money in the bank and deserve my reputation as the family's tight-fisted penny-pincher. I save pennies, clip coupons, and reseed my Johnny jump-ups. And I get a kick out of two-for-one restaurants.

In fact, I've created my own two-for-one plan: an extra afternoon movie after paying for one admission. At the multiplex, I saunter out at the end of one film and slip into the beginning of another. Plenty of room. The ushers never make a peep.

This changed a few weeks ago when I visited a nearby multiplex where reruns of favorite oldies are shown and saw "The Ten Commandments." Suitably uplifted, I headed for the lady's room, and as I came out, I noticed a long line for a rerun of "Pinocchio," one of my all time favorites. The crowd was huge, animated, maybe eight deep, snaking back farther than I could see. I decided to stay put in the bathroom, peeking out until the crowd started moving. Then I swiftly folded into the beginning of the line, with as much nonchalance as I could muster.

All of a sudden, a wiry young man in a yellow turtleneck moved swiftly toward me. A slim girl with red hair followed him. He had lively brown eyes and tiny glittery teeth. Did he know me? He appeared to be smiling, or was it a grimace? I smiled back, when unexpectedly he pushed a wagging finger in my face, and spat out in a raspy voice, "Shame on you, lady. I've been watching. I'm onto you. I've been studying your filthy tactics."

I was startled. Looking him over closely, I noticed that he needed a shave. His breath smelled of garlic. His expression was feral. Funny that I hadn't noticed this before. Tightly pursing his lips, he looked over my head and gestured to the others behind me, some of whom were already staring curiously.

"The gall of this woman, folks," he pointed to me and yelled to them, "sneaking in front of all you honest people waiting your legitimate turn!"

I turned around. Sure enough, at least forty pairs of accusing eyes were on me. My chin began to tremble.

"Now, Ziggy, dear," the redheaded girl cooed soothingly, as I stood mute and aghast, "take it easy – your blood pressure." She gently patted his wide shoulder and whispered to me, "His jail warden job puts him under a terrible strain. He's on medication." She awarded me a sweet wink. "Now, dear, leave this poor woman alone. She doesn't mean any harm."

"Yeah, Ziggy. Stop harassing that lady," called a woman's voice.

"Stop the abuse, Ziggy!" chanted several female voices.

"No way," he called back. "No fucking way." He waved a fist. "This woman is a criminal. She needs a lesson." Someone in the crowd applauded.

A faraway voice yelled, "Right on, Ziggy."

Trembling, I mentally began reviewing the Ten Commandments. Was this a sign that God was angry with me? My stomach tightened.

Opening my mouth, I could only emit a squeaky croak. What could I possibly say? I was guilty, caught and humiliated before this mob, all of whom could possibly turn on me, God forbid.

Returning to my childhood training, I reviewed a plausible alibi. I considered pretending to be hearing-impaired and signing to everyone with a sugary smile. Could I claim sadly, in a near-whisper, "The oncologist has given me less than a week."

I looked over the accusing crowd, now pushing us against the barrier. Ziggy screeched a pronouncement, "Go back, lady, back to where you belong." I heard the deep rumble of the other angry voices.

Then it happened. Like a bolt from the blue, I blurted out, "Walt Disney was my grandfather."

The crowd hushed. Someone said. "Wow."

I looked up at the ceiling where a mammoth plastic chandelier glittered brazenly. Tearful, I wailed, "I miss my Grandpa." Someone handed me a Kleenex.

As the ushers opened the double doors, I rushed to the front of the line. Turning back to the crowd, I looked up solemnly at the chandelier, whispered "Grandpa," then led everyone in.

My panic was swiftly returning. I rushed down the aisle and claimed a choice seat.

God forgive me. Mr. Disney forgive me. Grandpa, forgive me.

I wondered if someone intended to call the manager. I slipped down further in my seat and prayed.

An old woman came up to me and asked for my autograph.

"Your grandfather was a genius." she beamed. I nodded sadly and scribbled "Disney" on her ticket stub.

The lights dimmed. The audience hushed.

THE LADIES

Before I found the door to the western ladies restroom at Pahlavi University, named for Mohammed Reza Pahlavi, the Shah of Iran, I feared that it didn't exist. Mideastern toilets are flush to the ground, and my arthritic knees simply don't permit a squat. Would my full bladder have to wait in discomfort until I returned to my small bare apartment, shabby but thankfully outfitted with both a western and eastern toilet?

When I queried, I was assured by the Dean of the English Department that it existed and cheered when I found it, yet puzzled that its sign was in Farsi. Why not English, since it was after all, the English Department? I would be teaching literature in English to reluctant, budding engineers. At least there was a toilet that considered my needs.

It was dark in the western restroom as I slowly opened the door. Squinting, I saw in a corner of the dank little room a cobwebbed bucket and a mop. When I opened the door fully, which lit the little room a bit, I saw hundreds, perhaps thousands of tiny mice gaping at me with worried eyes.

I quickly shut the door. Was I hallucinating? I opened the door again. Many of the mice had vanished, and the last were skittering away to only Allah knew where. I was left bug-eyed and trembling, staring at a tall dusty western toilet, a bucket and a musty mop.

A few minutes later, I sauntered into my classroom to meet my first group of students. The room was large and bare, painted a sickly white, with an extraordinarily high ceiling and a wall of filthy windows.

Smiling nervously, having relieved myself, I walked swiftly to the front of the room to a large dented metal desk and balanced myself precariously on a tiny rickety stool in front of the desk, facing thirty grinning young men. They looked cheerful, almost giddy. At once they applauded. I had no notion why, but bowed my head and said thank you, "*Merci*," a common French word for thank you in Iran.

One of the students arose and walked to my desk, presenting me with a gaily wrapped and ribboned box. "Please open our present," he whispered in English. The box contained a roll of toilet paper, an item absent in the ladies. I was equally embarrassed and sincerely grateful to be among friends.

THE NEW YORK PERSIAN TAXI DRIVER

Taxi! Grand Central Station, please. I see by your identification that you're Iranian. Mahmood Kadjhavi. "*Hale shoma, Mahmood!* How are you, Mahmood? Yes. I speak a little Farsi, and you are my first Persian taxi driver in Manhattan!"

Yes, I lived in Shiraz in 1977 and 1978. Taught at Pahlavi University when Mohammed Reza Pahlavi, the Shah, was the Shah. I used taxis all the time in Shiraz. Once in a while I even hitched rides on the backs of motorcycles. Crazy, huh? In the early morning I would hail a taxi to Pahlavi University, where I taught Engineering students English Literature. We were amid a horrendous student revolution, which was frightening. The male students didn't want female students in their classes. They threatened the girls for wearing western clothes, warning they would throw acid in their faces! Ironically, my lectures were about the horrors of mob violence. One of my students threw a chair inches over my head, and then crashing out the window while I was lecturing. I don't think he was listening.

What a time that was! I can picture myself now, standing at the curb of Zand Avenue, near the statue of the great poet, Ferdosi, and waving an arm, calling out "*Adabiat! Adabiat!* School of Humanities!" The taxi driver would stop, and I'd squeeze in amidst too many other bodies.

At the beginning of my stay, I confused yes with no. The Iranian head motion for no looks like an American yes – a bob of the head. Yes looks like no, and no looks like yes. Until I figured it out, the cabbies would yap, "No go Adabiat. No. No." They'd pull me out of the cab while I thought they were bobbing their heads yes.

Wow, Mahmood. Close call! Allah must be watching over you, cutting in front of that truck. And your zigzag streets are pushing up my fare. You are *taroofing* me, tricking me, like a regular New York cabbie.

After a while I was hired by the Iranian Police Department to teach traffic signals in English. Good money. I'd taxi from the University in the late afternoon to the old section of town, near the bazaar and the big Mosque. Ever been there? All that chanting and tape-recorded calls for prayer from the minaret. The air thick and smoky with baking flatbread that Kasha vendors sold to long lines of whispering women in black *chadors*.

In the big downtown Police Station, I pretended not to hear the screams coming from the other rooms. I sat on a platform, like a dais, on an elaborate chair at a huge desk at the head of the classroom facing 30 smiling police officers. They were so open faced, like sweet young kids. Much nicer than the rebelling engineering students who yearned for the Shah's downfall, the return of tradition, and that lunatic, Khomeini.

The police treated me like the Empress Farah. They told me about their wives, their children, what they had for dinner. I was surprised that everyone ate the same thing. Tons of rice, cucumbers, zucchini, yogurt, chicken, tea. I was surprised that marrying first cousins was common – keeps wealth in the family – and that middle-aged men, even doctors, lawyers, single until late in life, then married twelve-year-old girls!

But those police were good to me. If I coughed, Sargeant Mo-
hammedtaghi slipped out for flavored ices. If I sneezed, a box of pink
Kleenex would mysteriously appear at my desk. We rarely talked
about traffic, stop and go, left turn, right turn. We wanted to know
about each other's lives. Were they spies, you ask? Only Allah knows.
I fantasized I was an ambassador of good will. Once I mentioned a
yen for pistachios. The next day I really needed a taxi to lug a bale of
them home.

I miss that year, that dangerous place, as bad as NYC, almost.
Different dangers. No muggings or robberies, but a man could get a
hand lopped off for stealing a rug or pinching someone's bottom. I
miss being forty-something in exotic Shiraz, City of Poets and Roses.
We're at Grand Central? Already?

Goodbye, Mahmood. *Khoda Hafiz.* May God protect you.

A CERTAIN
TYPE OF GIRL

With children, you can never be too careful. Let them stray, you might lose them forever. My Joseph, a voice like an angel; he could be a cantor. And a quiz kid too, no less; he could be a rabbi. I tried to keep him close to home. I even prayed to God that he should never get in the clutches of that type of girl.

You know the type I'm telling you? A sneaky piece of fluff hiding a secret plan behind a smile sweet as butter. Long eyelashes. Swaying hips. God help me.

My Joseph, he was a *boychik*, innocent, which is why I didn't allow him out of town for college. Besides, Brooklyn College was good enough for his brother. Why should he be the big shot?

An obedient, respectful boy, my Joseph. He'd babysit his sister after school so I could take care of Mama. Arthritis – how that woman suffered. She'd beg me, "Don't put me away." I'd never disgrace her by sending her to a "home."

I used to worry, God forbid, what happened to Mama would happen to me. Bedridden, needing my children to take care of me. I always counted on my Joseph; he would take me in.

I know everyone says it should be the daughter who takes care of the mother, or the oldest son. But my oldest, Arthur, has a wife from hell, healthy and Jewish, thank God, but what a mouth. And my beautiful daughter, Melanie? I wouldn't allow her to burden herself. Besides, she has to work. She's on her feet all day in the glove department at Henri Bendel. Her husband, Mr. Pretty Boy, doesn't make a decent living. I told her she should marry a doctor. She said they made a beautiful couple. Where do children get their ideas?

Men are pushovers when it comes to that flirty type. They can't help it. It's their nature. Which is why our people send the boys to *cheder* to study Hebrew. *Daven* three times a day. Keeps away temptation.

Girls like that type? Plenty at the Shadyside Nursing School where I studied to be a nurse. Nogoodniks, floozies, looking for a rich doctor. Hanging around the hospital after their shift. Where do they get their nerve?

My husband, Sam, was so proud when Joseph got in to Harvard Medical School. "Sam," I said, "We're in for trouble." My Sam, he didn't listen. Men don't think ahead. That's why there are wars.

Harvard is where Joseph met her. She was working three jobs and getting a nursing degree at the same time. Three jobs? You couldn't tell me she wasn't looking. Receptionist at the dormitory? She got to look over the whole field.

My Joseph was smitten. "Wait till you meet her, Ma. She's from New Jersey."

"New Jersey?" He says it in a whisper, as if New Jersey was the Promised Land.

So, what's wrong he couldn't find a nice girl from Brooklyn? Margie Freedman? Margie takes her mother shopping for *Shabbos* every week. Drives her to the doctor.

Then he brings the girl to visit. Sweet as honey. She knew all the tricks. And what kind of parents would let a twenty-year-old child visit a boy in a strange city? That girl had her teeth in my Joseph's neck!

My father-in-law used to say to my mother-in-law, "You can't stop the wind."

My mother-in-law? The woman was crazy. When my Sam said he was going to marry me, she screamed and she threw a sterling silver tray out the window.

You ask me, she had a fixation on her own son. No one was good enough. She wanted a rich family for him. My family was poor. You'd think it was my fault, but I was the first in my family to make something of my life. My mother-in-law should have been proud. A nurse marrying a rich doctor. Who says it isn't perfectly natural?

EVERYONE KNOWS

It's true. I am fearful and shy. Ask my father. "Just like Mother," he'd say. "Talented." "Entertaining." "Actress." "Artist." "Engaging." All an act. Deep down, pretense and pancake makeup stripped away, your Mother was fearful and shy just like you".

Fearful and shy. Didn't I sit silent with all the other mothers at the PTA, hyperventilating, stuttering, swallowing air, with knees trembling?

Actually, everyone knows I'm fearless and bold. Ask my husband. "Bold," he'll say, "like her mother. Requesting the largest hotel room facing the ocean. Quietest corner at the restaurant. Pushing into executives' offices with complaints, advice and suggestions."

I am bold. Didn't I spend a summer alone with my camera in Mexico City on buses crammed with staring chickens? A year in Shiraz, Iran, teaching traffic signals in English to fawning police lieutenants who offered me vanilla ices when I coughed? Their pretty wives baked me luscious pistachio pastries, as if I were Princess Soraya.

Everyone knows I'm difficult and rebellious. Ask my brother. "Just like Mom," he'd say. "Two peas, both scorning convention. Loudly yawning with their mouths wide open in my sedate country club. Embarrassing! Weirdo friends with weirdo hairdos."

Yes. I'm eccentric. It is true.

It's true that I'm traditional like Mom. Linen napkins, tall candles on the dinner table. Roses and tomatoes in the garden. Wallpaper with tiny blue flowers. Ask Mom. Cozy on the couch under a huge, framed hand-colored photo of our family, she and I study picture albums together. Mom points to a snapshot of herself and cries, "Look, it's you!"

I'm selfish. "Inconsiderate," says my sister-in-law. "Careless and narcissistic like her mother. Does she ever help with the dishes? Does she write thank you notes or send birthday presents?"

I love shopping, choosing high new feathered hats and slippery silk scarves for myself. It's also true that I'm easy company. An attentive listener. Tactful and well-intentioned. A loyal friend. Kind.

Ask me.

HUSBAND AT HOME

Retirement suits him, spotless lab coat,
weary Talbot ties closeted away.
He putters in Levi's, no-name sandals,
hums "Cara Nome" with Alexa,
prunes double-ruffled fuchsias,
tends trailing bougainvillea.

Office memos, check-ups,
growth charts, harried nurses,
vaccinations, countless phone calls,
squalling spit-up babies gone.
All those other families' frantic mothers.

Years ago, a social worker warned,
don't surrender the kitchen.
Let him vacuum, suck daddy long legs
out of bedroom corners.

Dish detergent bubbles
the kitchen sink, warm water
splashes, my reclaimed lover
washes our Noritaki dinner plates.

A sweet-cream smile, a sigh,
while filing them to dry, neat
as alphabetized office charts.

Dinner done, familiar creamy kiss,
a moment's linger, then in a rush,
he ushers me out the kitchen door,
wishing solitude.
Football.

THE MODEL

"You've got your mother's looks, thank God!" Dad tells me. Mom was Miss Jersey City in her day – tall, like me, high cheekbones, but with sky blue eyes I'd die for. Mine are boring brown.

Yeah, Miss Jersey City, Mom's only claim to fame. She had high expectations, but she married Dad, who wouldn't let her out of the house.

"You could have been famous, Mom."

"Yeah." Mom sighs. "Coulda, shoulda, woulda."

Me? I'm a model in the garment district. Until last year I lived at home in a two bedroom one bath with a smelly maroon carpet and mustard colored walls. Mom complained when I moved out that I abandoned her, but I couldn't take the booze and butts.

College? No way! I never knew anyone who went. A miracle I graduated high school since I was hardly ever there. Secretarial school? Who'd want to go if she could be a model?

My boyfriend, Charlie, wants to protect me. He calls daily to check up when the buyers ask me to dinner, which is part of my job. Charlie asks where, trails me there and back, making sure all I do is dinner.

Mom says forget Charlie, he's a loser, like Dad. I should hook up with one of the buyers, but they're too old for me and too short.

"Yes, Charlie drinks, but nothing like Dad," I tell Mom. "He's only soused on weekends."

ZONES OF GRAY

I focused my Graflex, steadily mounted on a tripod, as my wife rolled her eyes while hugging her dimpled knees, posing in profile at Bridal Veil Falls, pensive under the tall trees.

I hung the photo on the wall. Now my former wife, exposed at Yosemite in black and white fiber-based, acid-free paper. Archival.

Note the background textures: carved barks of ponderosa, giant sequoia shadows, patterns reflected in a mirrored lake – the contrasts; varied gray tones.

We photographers call them zones.

Vivid color excited her, quickened her heart, melted all rational senses. Perhaps an enzyme gushed when she fled with a pastel painter. She left me the child.

I shifted my professional path and discovered power over color wavelengths, and thus altered my daughter's perception. To ensure her protection, I snipped off a mere slice of spectrum, withholding all malevolent hues.

It's irreversible. My daughter will remain achromatic.

She is now grown, delights in each gray zone, marvels at highlights, at scale. In shadows, entranced, she seeks every detail.

GOD KNOWS

I'm used to my husband being the spokesman for the family because he's a doctor, so his opinions are respected. A brilliant man, my husband, but quiet, modest. I dress him in elegant clothes from New York City, the finest shops. I iron a clean white shirt each day. Fresh pajamas every night.

I don't shop that way for myself or the children. Kaufman's in Pittsburgh is good enough for us. Well, it's true that I did shop in New York for my Arlene, my daughter. A beautiful girl. She could have had anyone she wanted. She could have married into the richest Jewish family in Pittsburgh. A beautiful girl and her father a doctor. That noodnik she chose? Mr. Pretty Boy? It broke my heart.

So you can see why I wouldn't be the opinion giver. Not with a professional man like my husband to say his piece. Not that I don't have opinions. Ask the Sisterhood of the *Shul*. The Hadassah. When I'm with my friends, my opinions are respected. Not only because my husband is a doctor, but I myself was a nurse, which is how I got my husband.

My whole family celebrated when I became a nurse. No one else had a profession. My sisters respected me. In fact, they've been a little afraid of me because I hold very strong opinions, but my husband being the spokesman, I keep them to myself.

Mama had ten children but she disowned two, so I don't count Zelkie and Jake as my brothers any more. They married *shiksas*.

Mama told me when I see them on the street, I should turn my head. It's God's rule.

I used to think, God forbid, it could happen to me. One of my children could marry outside the faith. The punishment for disobedience to God is very severe. The whole community will cast you out, and who wants to be alone? Living by His law and in His love and approval is the only way. Mama taught me this. I have lived that way always. I taught this to my children, but they weren't paying attention.

My children, Oy! How can I explain to God what they've done? Two have married Christians. My oldest married a Jewish woman first, rich, pretty, but what a mouth and she hated me, snubbed me on the street, was jealous of my Arlene.

I said to my son, "Listen, it's all right, at least she's Jewish, so my grandchildren have a Jewish mother." But he disgraced me. He left his Jewish wife and married an Episcopalian twenty-two years younger with three blond babies. What are people saying about me?

Forgive me, God. I have decided not to disown my children. No, Mama, I won't disown my children. After all, my gentile son-in-law is a genius at repairing things. He fixed my TV. And my new daughter-in-law plays the trombone and is very clean. Her home is immaculate.

I believe God has forgiven me. You know, maybe God's rules are like a multiple choice test with a trick answer. Who knows? Maybe I passed the test.

END OF SUMMER

The sweet smell of hay wafts into the open kitchen window. It's the first Sunday in July. Scrubbed and combed, I'm dining with the Davis family on their dairy farm, my second summer here, a planet away from our dark Brooklyn apartment.

I could hardly wait for school to let out and my parents to drive me to West Milton. My heart thumped and jumped all the way. I love it here. Two joyous months.

In Brooklyn, nothing makes sense. What's the point of school? Who needs logarithms? Farm life is purposeful. At the dairy farm I'm needed. Planting seeds for corn we will eat. Squash, peppers, beans. Feeding chickens, gathering eggs, milking cows.

I have my own bedroom. Yellow curtains with blue flowers match the quilt the farmer's wife sewed. She is teaching me how to crochet.

Today I look across the dinner table at kind, worn faces. Today I am part of this family and wish I could live here year around.

Suddenly, a strange noise. The farmer struggles up from the table with a croaking sound from his throat. He clutches his neck, falls to the floor.

I am sent outside. Sobbing, I hear snatches of hushed conversation in the kitchen. An ambulance whines. I am told to pack my things. My parents are on their way.

I am silent on the drive back to Brooklyn. Dirt-streaked tears run down my face. Summer is over, and it's not yet the Fourth of July.

SHE TALKS IN CLASS

When the kindergarten teacher sent me home with a note, I thought Mother would be proud. I was barely five and I could read it to her.

"Sondra talks in class."

Mother stood shivering on the lawn, bare legs wide apart, high shoulders held tight. Her checkered kerchief whipped in the November wind.

My brother sat nearby in his stroller, blanketed, mittened, watching Mother swiftly swing her right arm, her hand slapping my cheek hard. I blew down.

Brother looked surprised. He didn't cry, but his mouth squeezed out a small black o.

I didn't cry either, fallen on the frozen lawn. My breath was gone. When my short gasps and gulps quieted, I knew it was dangerous to talk.

> Surviving in silence,
> the poet, voiceless,
> pens her song.

THE OLD TRIBAL WOMAN

*T*he old woman looks directly into my camera's lens. She squats at the edge of the rug she is weaving and then gazes up at me, and we meet eye to inquisitive eye. Her eyes, dark and shiny as black olives, are alert, her gaze, arresting. Is she as curious about me as I am about her? Does amusement hide in that impassive stare? Contempt?

"Who are you, western lady with your black box and strange blue men's trousers? Your hands with their painted nails are useless. I scorn your soft hands. You know nothing of my people's life. I know no other. I wove this rug, a Kashgai, named for my people. The wool comes from the sheep that travel with my tribe, along with camels, goats and mules. They are our family. We shear the wool, cut it, dye it with the plants and berries of the fields. Each year we travel with our animals to find land to graze. We camp in the hills of Shiraz in the winter and travel to Esfahan each summer. I work every day at the carpet weaving school, weaving these rugs. It's been my work since I was seven years old and my hands were tiny. See how strong they are?"

I look at her knobby hands with their round-as-coins nails. They are competent, assured, stained from wool dye. The heels are enlarged. These working hands were probably quick in her youth, but now the enlarged joints look painful and arthritic. Her walnut skin is worn as a used paper bag.

"Our heritage is the fields and hills of Russia, Turkey, Afghanistan. We've lived the nomadic life for centuries. I was pretty as a girl. My ten children look more like their father. I thank Allah for giving me eight sons. All my life I have worked and have produced many beautiful rugs, and eight strong sons. I will continue working as long as Allah wishes."

She looks down and returns her full attention to her craft, leaving us both alone with our thoughts.

REHEARSAL

"Do it again."

"Class 5B2 …"

"No. No, Roberta. Louder! You aren't projecting."

"Class 5B2…"

"I still can't hear you." My Mother pounds her little fists on the kitchen table. "Listen Roberta," she says, "don't aggravate me." She looks at her watch. "Time is running out. It's Tuesday already and on Friday morning you'll be standing on the stage in that big auditorium in front of the whole school." Her left eyelid twitches.

"Everyone's eyes will be on you." She rises from the kitchen chair, walks over to the stove, her narrow high heels clicking across the linoleum. She lights a cigarette with a wooden match. She puffs her cigarette and removes a tobacco speck from her tongue.

"Your first time ever in a school play, Roberta. First time in your life you're in something."

That's not true, I say to myself. *What about the fifth grade spelling bee last month? I won it, didn't I?* Spelling is my favorite subject. I want to say, "Listen, Mother, I was in something. I won the spelling bee. Don't you remember?"

I remain silent.

Mother rubs her ankle. She takes off her left shoe and examines the callus on her heel. Then, she looks up at me, "Everyone will be there: The whole school: The teachers, the parents, even the principal."

Her face is very serious. She whispers, "This is an important event, Roberta; the impression you make..." Her eyes brighten. "It's like a debut!"

I put on my most solemn face and look down at the skinny trail of baby ants crossing the kitchen linoleum heading for the refrigerator. My elbow itches. I spell debut in my head. "D-E-B-U-T, debut. What's a debut?" I wonder, but I don't ask.

"Will you please pay attention?" Mother calls out. 'Why are you looking at the floor? Look up at me." I look up into her eyes.

"Now, stand up straight and tall, as if you were balancing a book on your head. And smile at the audience." I force a smile. "Speak slow and clear and loud." Mother yells "loud."

"Wait a minute." Her tone softens. "Please push your hair out of your eyes. O.K. again."

"Class 5B2 ..."

Thank Goodness the school play is Friday, just a few more days away. We've been practicing every day after school, over and over. Mother insists we need to rehearse an hour a day, and I'm not even in the play. I've told her again and again. "Look, Mother," I said, "I'm not an actress and I don't want to be an actress. I'm not really in the play. I'm the presenter. I say, 'Class 5B2 Presents...' Only twenty-three words. Ask Miss Heymont."

Miss Heymont told me my role is to introduce the play. *It's a very important part*, she said. *It's the first impression.* She patted my shoulder. She said everyone would pay attention to me before the play begins. She said she chose me for the introduction because I am a dignified and serious girl. *It will set the right mood*, she said. Just before the play starts, I am to go up to the podium and when the audience settles down, I give a big smile, and then do the introduction. Then I point to the curtain as it rises and call out, "Let the play begin."

The lights will come up and Harvey Lyons will march downstage, followed by the other students. He'll beat the drums and lead the pageant in a march around the stage while I tiptoe silently down the steps and back to my seat.

"The whole school will be watching, Roberta." Mother's voice is breathy and urgent and squeaky – the way she sounds when she's getting all riled up, so I know not to interrupt or contradict or say even one word. Only Daddy knows how to calm her when she gets that way.

"All the teachers, everyone's mother..."

The truth is, Mother is the one who wants to be an actress. She tells me that over and over, like she's memorized the words.

"Moss Hart, the famous playwright said he'd write a part for me in one of his plays. He said I had a natural talent." Then she starts crying. I get her some Kleenex and she blows her nose. "I should never have married your father. We were both too young."

"Can we stop practicing now, Mother?"

"No. At the Actor's Workshop, they told us that every part in a play is equally important. When you're up there on stage, you have a serious responsibility. It really matters that you do your role perfect as you can, Roberta. Otherwise, you'll throw the other actors off and ruin everything."

On the night before the play, Mother brings a large white box into my bedroom. "Surprise! A present for you." I am truly surprised. Presents, except for birthdays and Hanukkah, are rare. In the box is a white middy blouse with puffed sleeves.

"It'll make your shoulders look broader. You've got narrow shoulders, like Daddy." She sounds pleased.

And a bright new red tie.

"The perfect shade for your skin tone." She sits next to me on my bed, smiles, and touches my cheek oh so gently. It frightens me a little, so I jump back. "You'll wear rouge tomorrow. A performance is special. Now, you must get to bed early so you'll be fresh as a daisy for tomorrow."

I can't sleep. I doze off and then awaken startled, gulping air. What if I forget my words and must stand onstage frozen, everyone staring at my puffed sleeves? My stomach tightens. I run into the bathroom, lock the door, and stand facing the mirror.

"Class 5B2," I say into the mirror: My voice is squeaky. My face looks worried. My chin trembles. *Take a good deep breath, and say it again*, I tell myself.

"Class 5B2 presents a Thanksgiving pageant," I call into the mirror, pushing out a big wide grin. There is knocking at the door.

My father calls, "You all right, sweetheart?"

"I'm fine, Daddy." I notice my teeth are small and white and even, just like Mother's. Same high cheekbones. Same straight brown hair. Same smile.

I wish Mother smiled more.

I smile again and whisper into the mirror, "Maybe I'll be an actress too."

SMELL

It's over three hours, and I can't find it. Every time I open the refrigerator, an awful smell fills the kitchen and floats down the hallway, invading every room. All the while, my husband sits in his Barcalounger reading, watching PBS, wearing earphones and conducting "The Sorcerer's Apprentice." My husband prides himself on his ability to do several things at once.

At the refrigerator again, I try to sniff it out. Maybe it's cheese. Limburger? No. It's securely wrapped. Milk past its expiration date? No. It isn't milk.

"Isn't that smell putrid?" I ask my husband as I enter the living room.

"Huh?"

"It wasn't the milk."

"What wasn't milk?" He's reading the obituaries. "Did you know that Christopher Kelly died?

"Oh! How terrible!"

For a change, I've no idea who he's talking about.

"The first oboe of the Minneapolis Symphony. What about milk?"

"That smell." I scan the coffee table, sniff into the vase of Mr. Lincoln roses. "You don't smell anything?"

I don't expect yes. My husband doesn't like getting involved.

"No, I don't. It's my allergies. Well, look at this. Florida is flooding. The divorce rate is down."

My husband is a born "Information Please." Since our honeymoon he's fed me a barrage of random data, relentless as the NASDAQ ticker.

"Speaking of milk," he asks, "when's lunch?"

"After I track down that smell."

"Why are you harping?" he says, "I don't smell anything."

Ironically, I've a nose for smelling. I once worked in a perfumery measuring milligrams of aromatic chemicals, creating Joy, Charlie, and New Car Smell. Blindfolded, I can distinguish Lilac from Lily.

"Fidelity Magellan is down," my husband announces. "Sunset Boulevard" is coming to Cleveland."

Why is he telling me Cleveland when we're in San Francisco? I groan, dreading the task of emptying the fridge shelf by shelf.

Suddenly, an incredible idea hits me. Exorcism!

"In my seductive voice, I say, "Come. Let's hold hands around the table."

"Why?"

"Trust me. Afterward I'll make a sumptuous lunch."

Hungry, pocketing his Kleenex, he sits at the table.

You are a great sport," I tell him with a hug. We sit, hold hands, shut our eyes.

"Sniff," I whisper.

"They did this once on Nova," he tells me.

"Sniff," my voice commands. Sighing, he complies.

Eyes closed, we sit quietly. The table jumps. There's a rattling noise.

"It's working," I whisper.

Suddenly, I hear a melodious voice.

"Oh, sweet spirits," it calls. I look up. It's my husband. "Lift that smell," he sings out, trancelike, "Float it gently out the window. Away. Away."

61

A sweet breeze wafts through the kitchen. He opens his eyes. "What happened?"

"It's gone," I tell him. "The smell is gone."

"Really?"

"And you did it! I'm astonished."

He claps his hands. "Hooray!"

After lunch, he is ready to return to the newspaper when we hear bellowing next door. It's my neighbor. We lean out the window to hear.

"What's that Gawdawful smell?" she wails, "Came from nowhere." She calls to her husband. "Do you suppose it's the cheese?"

"Smell?" he replies, "I don't smell a thing."

MY LIFE IN A NUTSHELL

I am in Brooklyn on a Prospect Park pony, staring at my father's Rolleiflex, round-eyed and alert. Both the pony and I are two years old and named Sandy. We both wonder where we are going.

Me and Johnny Vaccaro empty the refrigerator and leave the contents on the kitchen floor. He tells my mother I did it and I get whipped. I decide to poison Johnny.

When everyone is asleep, I pick off all my chicken pox and throw them into the blizzard out my bedroom window.

I am gleefully waving the 5th grade spelling bee prize. Mrs. Shreiber's fat manicured hand squeezes my narrow shoulder as she forces a smile. She and I have hated each other since she called me a liar and a cheat and I told my mother, who told the principal. My middy blouse is ablaze with the prizes from my four previous wins: World War II pins commemorating our brave fighting men. I wear a soldier, sailor, marine, and coast guard pin. Mrs. Shreiber stands ready to pin a WAC on me. I sport a toothy grin.

I am sixteen and Stanley Deutsch calls me on the phone like I prayed he would. We end up going steady. I won't marry him because he has a dead tooth in front and is afraid of cars with a stick shift.

Bobby Gottlieb teaches me the backstroke in Morristown, New Jersey. His girlfriend before me wasn't pretty. I won't marry someone with low standards.

Al Lawrence breaks up with me in a long letter written in his tiny handwriting. I am heartbroken and turn to my studies. My college grades soar.

I decide to marry someone famous and smart. My husband has a well-shaped head and is not famous, but is quiz-kid smart. I star in the common-sense department.

I raise three amazing children and marvel at my creativity. Perhaps I'm an artist. I create lentil soup and salmon croquettes.

I go to Art School and become a photographer. I photograph apples, anemones, Mexican markets, and expose my daughter's knees on black and white panchromatic film. My daughter's knees are praised for their originality. I photograph the back of my husband's head.

Gradually, I become a grandmother of four. Three are tall and scholarly. The runt aspires to become a rock star.

We go to Iran for a year and I teach English and the History of American Photography at a Graduate School in Shiraz. I share my office with a hollow-eyed young man. He dresses in black and holds hushed meetings in Farsi with somber, chadored women and skinny, bearded men. At my desk I read student essays and learn that sleeveless blouses are an abomination. I notice that when the jailed students return to class they have shaved heads and silly smiles. The soldiers in the exam hall point rifles at my trembling students.

Everyone flunks.

In Shiraz I lose my fear of mice and flying cockroaches. I bathe along with the laundry every Thursday afternoon.

On returning to California, I miss the deep rumbling of student demonstrations, families of five on a motorcycle, cool mirrored mosques, pistachios and chelo kabob.

My fear of mice returns.

We move to Connecticut where I get hired at Fairfield University.

My students are cheerful undergraduates with hefty SAT's. I don't even have a Masters degree. My friends say wow.

We stay ten years. No one shares my office. The History professor in the office next door writes stuffy detective stories and smokes a calabash pipe. My students call me Dr. Steinman. We miss California. We save up, quit our jobs and return to the West.

I acquire three major exotic diseases and lose my fear of public speaking. I decide to perform soliloquies, participate in poetry readings and write a play about my mother-in-law.

I draw a picture in chalk pastel of the yellow cherry plums in the tree outside my kitchen door. I draw the blue cherry plums overhanging the living room deck.

I take a long walk in a nearby empty parking lot hoping to find good-luck pennies. I find a quarter and a perfect round mirror in an ivory frame.

My husband takes a picture of my mother resting her head on my shoulder. She has lost her memory and doesn't know my name. Her white hair is dazzling. I tell her she looks like Albert Einstein. She tells me she is a genius. Her eyes are closed. I face the camera, smiling, round-eyed and alert.

ABOUT THE AUTHOR

I wrote my first story in Brooklyn, where I was born. It was about Daisy, my dog, who died. I was in fourth grade and my teacher, Mr. Levy, was impressed. "Sondra, you are a writer." I was a writer? I was thrilled because I yearned to be a writer.

In the years that followed: Midwood High School, Wells College, Boston University, and Dominican University, no one commented on my writing. Disappointed, I was sad. Maybe I wasn't a writer. As I was nearing eighty, a wonderful poet and novelist, who taught classes in poetry and prose, delighted me with praise of my writing. I was a writer! She encouraged me to write a book, because, she said, I was such a good writer!

At that time I was a photographer, having spent the ten previous years at Fairfield University in Connecticut as an adjunct professor of darkroom photography. But digital photography had arrived and the darkroom was becoming obsolete. My job was in jeopardy. I didn't worry. Not a bit. Since fourth grade, didn't I yearn to be a writer?

I began attending lectures by writers, joined writing groups, writing clubs, joined performing groups, befriended other writers and enrolled in classes of poetry, prose, nonfiction, and playwriting, all in preparation for writing my book. For this book.

www.ingramcontent.com/pod-product-compliance
Lightning Source LLC
Chambersburg PA
CBHW030340020726
47493CB00004B/1343